TALES
FROM THE
TURRETS

JOAN LENNON

Illustrated by Scoular Anderson

Catnip

CATNIP BOOKS
Published by Catnip Publishing Ltd
14 Greville Street
London EC1N 8SB

This edition first published 2013
The Ferret Princess first published 2008
Wag and the King first published 2009
The Mucker's Tale first published 2010

1 3 5 7 9 10 8 6 4 2

Text copyright © Joan Lennon 2008, 2009, 2010
Illustrations copyright © Scoular Anderson 2008, 2009, 2010
The moral rights of the author and illustrator have been asserted

A CIP catalogue record for this book is available from the
British Library

ISBN 978-1-84647-160-5

Printed in Poland

www.catnippublishing.co.uk

Contents

THE FERRET PRINCESS

Chapter One

Trouble and Fuss

I was sitting up on the back battlements
in the spring sunshine, swinging my feet
over the edge and reading a book, when

the trouble arrived. Not that I *knew* it was trouble. Not right away. Not a clue. I was just sitting, trying to stay out of the way of any chores, thinking deep thoughts like, *I wonder what's for dinner?*

"PRINCESS! PRINCESS! WHERE ARE YOU?!"

When Fat Margaret yells, the sound carries from one end of our very small kingdom to the other. Pretending you haven't heard never works. I didn't even try. I just sighed and scooped up Jill, my ferret, from the sun-warmed stone, and wrapped her round my neck like a white fur sock. She sighed too, but she didn't bother to wake up.

Fat Margaret had me by the arm before I was halfway down the stairs. (She's called Fat Margaret because she's the skinniest woman you ever saw.

But that doesn't mean she's a weakling
– she's got a grip on her that'd be a
credit to a blacksmith.)

"Quick! On with your ceremonial
dress!"

"*What?!*" I squealed. She'd got me as
far as my room without much fuss, but
now I started to squirm as hard as a
worm in a beak. She *couldn't* be serious
about that dress!

"I can't wear *that*!" I wailed. "It's too
small, *and* it's ugly, and there's a great
big patch at the back where I scorched
it last winter!" (It was so cold that day
that I just kept backing closer and closer
to the fire . . .) "You mended it with
old *curtains*, for pity's sake – I *can't* wear
that!"

"And you can't wear anything else.
Oh, *don't* be difficult – you'll just have

to keep your back to the wall, or sit down a lot. With your lady mother ill, there's only *you* to receive guests, and there's only *this* to do it in!"

"Mngh? Mnmghmn?" I replied, which translates as "Guests? What guests?" My head was already deep

inside the dress, but that doesn't mean
I was happy about wearing it. Though
of course she was right. With my mother
unable to get up, there was only me to
act as hostess. (Everyone insisted she was
going to get better, but I tried not to
think about it much, because whenever
I did I got a tight feeling in my chest.)
There are *rules* for royal hostessing –
and one of them is that you can't greet
guests on behalf of an entire kingdom
wearing the same clothes you would to
muck out a stable.

But princesses don't muck out stables!
I hear you cry.

Well, yes they do, if they're poor
enough.

In those days, ours was the poorest
castle in the poorest kingdom as far
away up in the mountains as it's possible

to get. We were so out of the way, and so hard up, that mostly nobody paid us any heed at all. Conquerors *and* allies didn't really think we were worth the bother. They left us alone, and that suited us fine.

But there's always somebody down-on-their-luck and desperate enough to be jealous even of people like *us*. Somebody who hadn't managed to succeed in the big wide world out there. Somebody who thought it'd be a doddle, taking a bite out of a no-nothing kingdom, just for starters.

And, as it happened, two of them were waiting downstairs in the Grand Hall at this very moment.

So was I busy making clever political plans? Considering how to meet, greet and beat dangerous strangers at the game of diplomacy and power?

Not a bit of it. I was fussing about my *dress*.

As I said, I didn't have a clue.

Chapter Two

The Princess in the Picture

If you want to know what I look like, the best idea is probably to go see the painting. The one at the top of the main staircase. It was done a few years back, before my dad died, as a thank-you present from a travelling artist who stayed with us all that wet winter.

Yes, that's me. And I know what you're thinking.

"Doesn't she look like her pet!"

I admit it. Princesses come in all shapes and varieties, from the pink and fluffy, to the ravishing and regal, to the

15

older-than-your-auntie, and everything else besides.

I'm the ferrety sort, and so it's not surprising that they're my favourite animals of all time. (I learned everything I know about them from Warren, our ferreter. He's also our butler and cook and herald and ostler and Jack-of-all-trades and Master-of-pretty-much-all-of-them.)

Ferrets are betwixt-and-between creatures, not quite cats and not quite dogs. They have much more energy than sense, and they over-do *everything*. They love tight places, and sticking their noses where they don't belong, and making a mess of things out of sheer enthusiasm.

And that's pretty much *me*, too. I'm a two-legged, human, right-royal ferret. Well, except for the smell.★ And I don't jump up and down and pull on your breeches when I'm excited. But you get the idea.

★ The thing about ferrets and the way they smell? It's really not that bad – more musky than stinky. To us, I mean. To themselves, of course, *parfum de ferret* is lovely. Very nice indeed. Just right.

A word of warning, though. Don't go upsetting a ferret. If you do, you'll discover . . . well, just *don't*!

Chapter Three

My Big Entrance

"The news of the queen's illness must have got out," Fat Margaret said as she combed and twisted and generally beat my hair into submission. "They think we're an easy target now. These younger sons — they see their big brothers getting everything and they go all bitter and twisted — or else it's those second-rate nobles — they get greedy where they are, then they get thrown out, then they come looking . . ."

With the comb in her mouth it was harder to talk. I shoved in a question.

"How did they get over the border?"

Fat Margaret stuck the comb behind her ear.

"Don't be stupid, girl. You really think Old Albert could stop anybody who wanted to cross? Anyway, he wasn't on duty today. He was helping Leonard with the spring ploughing."

She gave the dress one more shake to make sure I was thoroughly into it, poked at my hair, and then shoved me in the direction of the Grand Hall.

"Warren will announce you," she hissed. "He's keeping them busy with food till we get there. I'll let him know you're coming." Then she raced off, taking the back way.

No short cuts for me, though. It was through the big double doors, and on down the full length of the great Grand Hall. It was a *long* room – which meant that there was a *lot* of time for our guests to take in all the details of me and my dress. Things like, how very un-pink, un-fluffy, un-regal and un-ravishing I was. Or how the

only jewellery I was wearing was an unconscious ferret round my neck. Or how old my dress was. Or just exactly how much too small it was. By the time I finally made it to their end of the room I was in such a panic, I felt certain the only question they could possibly have left would be, which room we'd taken the curtains from to patch the back of it with.

"The Third Spare Bedroom," I blurted.

There was a short stunned silence as the two noble newcomers and their dozen or so attendants all stared. Then Warren waded in with the introductions.

"Allow me," he croaked, coughed, and tried again. "Allow me to present Her Highness, the Princess Cecilia, daughter of Their Majesties Queen

Beatrice and the late King Horace of
this realm." He turned and bowed to
me. "Your Highness, may I introduce –"

He got no further. The taller of the two
strangers, lounging against the mantel,
cut across him as if he weren't there.

"I am Count Edward of Frore,"
he said, and then he sniffed. Then he
sniffed *again* and dabbed at his nose.
It's a definite aroma, ferret, but it was
obviously not one he'd met before.
While I tried to stop turning bright red,

he indicated, as an afterthought, the
other visitor not dressed as a servant.
"And, apparently, that's a Duke of . . .
someplace or other. We arrived at the
same time."

He would have used the same tone
of voice to say, "He wee'd on my shoe,"
but the Duke didn't seem to mind.

"Duke Ferdinand," he said, waving
a cold, cooked chicken leg and not

bothering to get up. "Of the Duchy of Dram. The, uh, story of your great beauty reached me, you see, and I had to, um, I had to . . . ah, come."

There was an expectant silence from everyone, but it seemed that was all the Duke of Dram had to say on the subject. The fact that my great beauty *was* a story didn't appear to trouble him. Then one of the Duke's company sidled over and whispered urgently in his ear.

"What?" said the Duke. "You say it's the mother who's the beauty? Oh well. Whatever."

He reached for a bit of chicken for his *other* hand, and carried on stuffing himself.

If he keeps going at that rate, I thought, *we'll have nothing left for dinner.*

Warren must have been thinking

along the same lines, because he
whisked the platter away between one
bite and the next, and quick as a cat,
hid it behind the chair. The Duke kept
chewing, but looked confused.

Not one of Nature's Mighty Minds, I thought to myself. *If I can't handle a wee Dukie-brain like this one, then I should be ashamed of myself.*

Before, I'd been so fussed about myself that I hadn't really *looked* at our guests carefully. But everything I was noticing about Duke Ferdinand now was making me feel more smug and confident by the moment. It seemed to me he was about as noble as my shoe, and as dangerous as that fake jewellery he was wearing – if he thought he could stroll into *my* kingdom and whisk it out from under *me* then he had another think coming and . . .

I realised Fat Margaret was nudging me, hard, with one of her unnecessarily sharp elbows. The Count was talking again.

"... and since your father the king,"
he was saying, "God rest him, died, I
know how much you and your lady
mother have missed a man's guiding
hand. Women running a kingdom isn't
quite the same, is it, and a *girl* ..."

I was all set to get mad, when I
looked him in the eyes – and instantly

I was too busy being scared. His eyes were cold, and hard, and hungry, and relentless, and . . . there was a horrible jolt in my brain as I realised, suddenly, completely, terrifyingly, the danger I was facing.

"When I heard of the queen's unfortunate illness, I felt obliged to pay my respects, along with my servants and all my loyal men-at-arms currently enjoying the hospitality of your peasants . . ." He shrugged his velvet shoulders and watched me, like some kind of malign spirit.

For one long horrible moment, my mind shut down. I felt like a rabbit in a hole, with nowhere to escape to.

The Count didn't move. He went on leaning against the mantelpiece. It was as if he knew exactly what I was feeling, exactly what I was thinking. He allowed himself a smile, and his teeth showed little and sharp.

"Er," I said desperately, and stopped. You could see he was getting pleasure out of watching me squirm, like a devil out of hell. Like an evil spirit. Like a . . .

And then, I remembered something. *Ye Byg Booke of Ghosties and Ghoulies* by Dr Sprout of Brussels (author also of the best-selling *Ye Noble Trials and Tribulations for the Gentrie*) – the book I'd been reading on the battlements that afternoon.

And all at once, I thought I could see a way out.

Chapter Four

The Pink and the Powerful

There was no time for hesitation – I plunged right in.

"Oh, *sir*," I cooed. "Thank you, thank you! We are so *grateful* to you and this other fine gentleman for showing an interest in little me and my little kingdom. So *few* noblemen these days have the *courage*, the *bravery*, the *fearlessness*, the . . ." I'd run out of nouns, but I acted breathless with admiration, instead. I'd seen my cousin Ermintrude do this many times with a great deal of success. "Two rival noblemen, ready to face the *horrors* of the Haunted Tower

– well, in Days of Yore, of course, there would have been *queues* of princes, eager to test themselves – but, sad to say, we live in decadent times . . ."

I could see Warren and Fat Margaret out of the corner of my eye. Both of them had their mouths hanging open.

"To spend an *entire* night in that *awful* place," I continued, desperately trying to signal to them without the Count or the

Duke seeing, "and so earn the right to rule my realm and perhaps, some day, my heart – to willingly choose *trial by ordeal* – oh, gentlemen, I am overcome." I put a hand to my forehead, and staggered a little. No effect.

"I said, *I'm overcome!*" I hissed to Fat Margaret, who jumped, shut her mouth, and, *at last*, rushed over to hold me up.

"Warren, get your mistress some water!" she barked. "You know how sensitive she is!" – though I could tell she was really thinking, *You know how crazy she is!*

"What are you talking about? What Haunted Tower? What trial by ordeal?" The Duke sat up straight, sounding panicky.

"Oh, sir, it's a fearsome place!" I squeaked, winking wildly at Warren as he handed me a cup, and repeating to myself, *Think fluffy! Think pink!* "Full of Evil Spirits! Rivals who seek to gain the kingdom must first pass the test – the *terrible* test of staying the night in the Tower and wrestling with *Fiends From Hell* until dawn. And all those who fail . . ." I dropped my voice for maximum drama ". . . *are never seen again.*"

The Duke was so agitated he even stopped chewing. "Nobody told *me* anything about F-f-fiends from Hell!" he stammered.

"Oh, yes, sir," said Warren, in his best butler's voice. "Well known that Tower is. Oh, ghastly things, sir, are told, of what

anyone courageous enough to stay there might meet — tentacley things, and slithery things, and headless things, and, and, strange noises, and er, gurglings, and . . ."

Fat Margaret took over. "And the hot fires of hell that burn you . . . that burn you . . ." she faltered.

". . . on the bum!" put in Warren helpfully.

Fat Margaret glared at him. "On the *nether regions*," she corrected primly. "I understand you can even catch a whiff of brimstone. On haunting nights. When the candidate fails, and is never seen again. Sirs." And she dropped a curtsey for good measure.

All this time, I'd been afraid to look at the Count, who was not a fool like the Duke. But now I did — and immediately wished I hadn't!

Something had shifted in the Count's face. It was as if he were seeing something else, some other scene from the past, that filled him with . . . what? Horror? Fury? It was like looking into the face of Death . . . until one of his servants touched him cautiously on the arm and he snapped back into the present again.

"You must take the test," I quavered. "Or forfeit my hand." *Will I get away with it?* I wondered. *Why on earth should they agree to any such thing?*

But my luck held. The Count, acting so snooty and superior he was in danger of disappearing up his own nose, nodded. The Duke, not to be left behind, jerked out a "Yes!" as well.

But there was something else on Duke Ferdinand's mind . . .

For some time now, his eyes had kept flicking nervously to my neck. He was making me self-conscious. I put a hand up and felt . . . Jill. I'd forgotten she was still there.

Something cracked for the Duke – it seemed he couldn't ignore what his eyes were telling him any longer.

"Your c-collar!" he stammered. "Is it . . . ? Is it . . . *breathing?!*"

"Oh, sir!" I cried, and I shrank back a little as if frightened. "What *do* you mean?!"

"Really, Duke, control yourself!" scoffed the Count. He turned and, not bothering to lower his voice, said to one of his servants, "Tell the men they'll be able to move into the castle tomorrow." He strode out of the Hall without a backward glance.

"Yes," said the Duke, trying to sound powerful too, but only succeeding in sounding like a duck. "Yes, tell *my* men that too. About, you know. Tomorrow."

Tomorrow, I thought as I watched him go. *But first we've got . . . tonight.*

Chapter Five

Scream?

Fat Margaret dragged me into an empty side room and slammed the door.

"Are you *crazy?!*" she hissed. "The Tower's not haunted! And even if it were – did you see the Count's face?! There's something ugly in that man's past, you can mark my words, something that came back to him when you started your nonsense about the Tower. What do you bet he did some awful deed in some similar test, maybe went berserk and killed everyone in sight, including the princess in question –"

"And her faithful hand-maiden too . . ." muttered Warren.

"Who are you calling a hand-maiden?!" spluttered Fat Margaret, wagging her finger indignantly in his direction.

Jill chose this moment to wake up. She lifted her head, and there was Fat Margaret's finger, wiggling about in front of her nose. So she bit it.

She let go right away, but not before Fat Margaret's remarkable lungs let out on enormous scream.

Almost immediately our unwelcome
guests and their followers fell into the
room, swords drawn.

"What is it? What's happening? Who
screamed?"

"Scream?" said Fat Margaret

innocently, but with her hands carefully behind her back so they wouldn't be able to see the blood. "What scream?"

"*I* didn't hear a scream," I added. I had *my* hands behind my back too. Mine were full of repentant ferret. "Unless – " I let my eyes widen as if in horror – "unless it's started already . . ."

"What's started already!?" quavered Ferdinand.

"Nothing. Nothing at all," I answered quickly. "Don't worry yourselves, gentle sirs. I'm sure it must have been . . . it must have been . . ."

"The wind!" said Fat Margaret. "Must have been." And she nodded emphatically.

At this point, Warren came in.

"Dinner is served," he announced.
"Allow me to conduct you to the
Dining Chamber, my lords."

"Oh good!" said Duke Ferdinand.

The Count held out an arm to me.
"Your Highness?"

I had to think fast.

"Um," I said.

"The Princess will be dining with her

ailing lady mother," said Fat Margaret quickly. "Of course."

The Count looked Fat Margaret up and down. You could tell he didn't much like what he saw. But he didn't say anything. He didn't need to. The man could *look* as much poison as a sackful of snakes. He just turned to me, bowed, and followed his rival out of the room.

Fat Margaret and I each let out ragged breaths.

"Nasty," she said. "Very."

I nodded.

"And you have a plan?"

I nodded again.

"I'll meet you in the Tower, then," she said, "as soon as I can make it. And I'd better bring Warren."

Chapter Six

Ulterior Design

Standing in the middle of the Tower Room, you had to admit it didn't look particularly sinister. Shabby, maybe, and in need of a good spring clean, but haunted?

Oh, dear.

What we had to work with was this: one big bed, three chairs, and a chest full of old clothes waiting to be turned into something else. There was a window with shutters that overlooked the moat far below, and, on the wall, an enormous threadbare tapestry that was so faded you couldn't tell what the

picture was any more. Next to it, there was a fireplace . . . and that was it.

Jill was exploring the bed, and I was on my knees in front of the chest, grubbing about in it for inspiration, when Warren and Fat Margaret arrived.

"Well?" she said.

"Ah," I said, "when I said I had a plan, I didn't exactly mean a *complete* plan . . ."

Fat Margaret snorted and started to pace. Warren started to prowl. And I started to throw clothes on the floor in an aimless sort of way.

Jill immediately left the bed and buried herself in the mess. Nose deep in the sleeve of an old gown, tail bushed up and wagging, she went blundering off across Fat Margaret's path, almost sending her flying.

Fat Margaret leapt out of the way, giving a startled squawk, then clapped her hand over her mouth.

"Oh, that beast did give me a fright!" she exclaimed crossly. "Now come *on*, you two – THINK!"

There was a short pause.

"Think," I said vaguely.

"Think," said Warren absently.

"YES!!" scolded Fat Margaret. "Stop being useless and help me figure out *how* on earth we are going to rig this room up in any way whatsoever scary enough to spook two grown greedy dangerous nasty . . . ARE YOU LISTENING TO ME?!?"

We weren't.

I was staring at Warren. Warren was staring at me.

"And we have . . . how many ferrets

in the busyness★ just now?" I asked, trying to sound casual.

Warren counted on his fingers. "There's Frank and Hob and Big Bob and Jeremy and Sable and Kevin, and Cynthia and Katie and Jenny and Pinkums, and Jill, of course, and wee Emily. That's twelve."

★A group of ferrets is called a busyness. Who says there's no truth in advertising?!

"A dozen ferrets," I said.

"That's right," he said.

"Should be enough," I said.

"I'll go fetch some treats," he said.

"WHAT IS GOING ON???" said Fat Margaret through clenched teeth.

I went over and patted her on the shoulder.

"Trust me," I said. "I'm a princess."

Chapter Seven

Trials and Tribulations for the Gentrie

When bedtime for the noblemen came,
Warren and I were out of sight, hidden
behind the tapestry. Nothing could
begin until they were asleep, but Duke
Ferdinand was so busy babbling that
that might not be for some time. He
kept boasting about how fantastically
fearless he was and then wondering if
the Tower really *could* be haunted, but
the Count didn't deign to answer him.
He didn't say anything at all until, in a
rare pause for breath by the Duke, we
heard his voice, low and cold.

"They'll pay for this."

Just four words – but they made my heart stutter.

They must have had an effect on the Duke as well, because he stopped rabbitting. Not long afterwards the candles were blown out and the bed creaked.

We waited. And waited. And waited.

The stillness seemed to go on forever until, finally, Warren peered out around the edge of the tapestry.

"All right," he whispered. "They're asleep. Let's go."

We tiptoed about in the dying firelight, laying out articles of clothing with the sleeves and legs tied at the ends, and tasty bits of food stuffed inside.

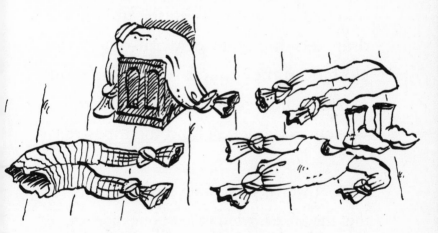

Some were on the floor. Some were on the chairs. I hung a gown from a hook behind the door and put treats in its pockets. It was long past ferret teatime, and even if it weren't, we knew full well that not one of our beasts could resist the challenge of a titbit, just out of reach, at the end of anything even remotely tunnel-like. There were eager scuffling noises from inside the chest, where the entire busyness of hungry ferrets had been hidden.★ As a final touch, Warren stirred up the fire and draped a thin piece of worn-out scarlet cloth from the mantel, so that the room was now bathed in a ghastly glow. Then we scurried back behind the tapestry,

★ Don't worry. It's a thing about ferrets that they like having at least one more of themselves in a space than will sensibly fit. Even so, don't try this at home.

flipping open the lid of the chest as we
passed, and MOANED!

The two noblemen sat bolt upright
in the bed. As their eyes snapped
open they saw, to their horror, strange
shapes racing about the room, lit by an
unearthly redness. The shapes chittered

and squeaked like wingless bats out
of hell – and then *disappeared!* In their
place, larger creatures appeared, with
oddly shaped bodies wearing tunics
and breeches and shoes
that juddered and
twitched, then
slithered about on
the floor in different
directions. In the doorway,
something wearing a dress
danced and swayed
wildly. Everywhere
there were headless
apparitions
falling apart in front
of their eyes and making
horrible muffled gargling
sounds . . .

"It's the demons!" shrieked the Duke. "They've come to get me!" And he tried to leap into the Count's arms.

Count Edward snarled and pushed him away. The Duke whimpered and dived under the blankets. The Count's face was twisted and his teeth showed in the strange light, but he showed no sign of budging.

It wasn't working! Instead of running out of the room yelling, one of them was so scared he was practically inside the mattress, and the other wasn't anywhere near scared *enough*. Warren and I looked at each other in desperation – what more could we do?

Then, amidst the demonic chuckling and chattering and writhing, we heard something else – another sound, one that was growing in volume all the time. It was a *hissing*, followed by a *bump, bump*.

The Count's eyes swivelled in his head, trying to locate this new horror. From the edge of the tapestry we did the same, because a hissing ferret is not a happy one. And then we spotted her.

It was Emily. She was the youngest of the busyness, barely more than a kit, and, in spite of having a heart full of courage, she was not very big and not very strong.

She'd managed to get herself completely tangled in an old pair of breeches, *and* she had run them and herself into a corner, *and* no matter how hard she thrashed and squirmed, she couldn't get at the treat and she couldn't get out. She just kept banging into the wall, getting more and more frustrated.

Then the Count did something we hadn't expected. He stood up – *and he was holding his sword!*

He must have had it in bed with him. Suddenly Fat Margaret's guess about the Count slaughtering princesses in the past seemed not so unbelievable. And, as luck would have it, this was the moment Emily finally made her escape. She'd managed to get her head out of the breeches. The first thing that met her eyes was a complete stranger, creeping towards her with a drawn sword.

She *screeched*.

It was a noise that made every adult ferret in the room freeze in its tracks. It was a noise that made the Duke of Dram burrow even deeper under the bedclothes, wailing as he went. But the Count –

– just kept on creeping. He was bending right over now, trying in the dim light to identify what it was he was seeing, there on the floor.

There was no chance he was going to get away with this.

There was a tremendous scrabbling
of claws and ripping of old clothes from
every part of the room. Some of the
busyness headed straight for Emily, got
her out of the breeches, scruffed her and
dragged her away to safety. The rest
turned their attention to THE THREAT.

As one, they leapt into the air and sank a multitude of needle-sharp teeth into that bit that sticks out the most, when a Count (or anybody else for that matter) bends way over . . .

They bit him right on *the Nether Regions!*

"Help! Help! My bum's on fire!" shrieked the Count. "*They got me!*"

Ferdinand peeked out from under the pillows. By now the Count was spinning round like a crazy thing, batting at his backside with a great flailing of bony arms and flapping nightshirt. It was impossible to *see* what was happening to him, but Ferdinand had no trouble with another of his senses.

"PEE-YEWWW!!" he gasped.

The Duke fell out of the bed and staggered back against the far wall, holding his sleeve over his nose and mouth and gagging.

"EUGGHHH! Heaven preserve us – it must be . . . IT'S THE STINK OF HELLLL!!" he gargled. With his free hand he began to fumble wildly with the shutters – he wrenched them open at last –

– and leapt straight out the window!

I *screamed*. I couldn't help it! I'm pretty sure Warren screamed too. That may have been the last straw for the Count – I don't know. Because then *he did it too!*

Nightshirt flapping, arms windmilling, and with a bunch of fully bushed-up ferrets attached to his backside like the tail to a comet, Count Edward of Frore staggered across to the window and *dived*.

Chapter Eight

What Happened Next . . .

Warren and I raced to the window and leaned out.

Far below, there was something thrashing in the moat. *Two* somethings,

which eventually floundered over to
the edge, dragged themselves out, and
ran off, gibbering, into the moonlight.
And then . . .

. . . the sound of delighted
chittering drifted up to us. There,
messing about in the water, as if
they went flying off tall towers
attached to strangers every
day of the week, were the
ferrets.

Warren let a whoop of relief and
raced off down the stairs to collect
them.

Smiling insanely, I set about doing
the same with the rest of the busyness.
Finding and bagging a lot of over-
excited ferrets is not the job of a
moment, but I managed it at last, just as
Warren returned.

I turned to him, happy and triumphant.

"And I found Hob, and Big Bob, and Cynthia and Jenny," he said. "Down by the moat. They're not hurt. Just a bit crazy. Like after a bath."

Then he paused, and the look on his face made me feel as if I'd swallowed my heart.

"And Frank and Sable and Jeremy and Emily – I've got them here,"

I said breathlessly. "They're fine – look – they're fast asleep already – it was just a game to them – really it was . . ."

He nodded. "And Katie and Pinkums were chasing Kevin about on the staircase as I came up." He stopped.

"And?" My voice sounded wrong.

Warren didn't seem to want to look at me.

"AND?" I shouted.

"It's Jill," he said. "Where's Jill."

Suddenly it was all more than I could bear. It had been just too long a day and too crazy a night and I'd almost killed two people and now it looked as if I *had* killed my best ferret-friend and it had all seemed like such a good idea at the time . . .

Suddenly I just wanted my mum.

Chapter Nine

The White One?

I blundered along the corridor with no
thought to how late it was, and piled
straight into Fat Margaret's skinny
arms. She was just coming out of my
mother's room. She took one look at me,
and said,

"Go on in with you then. She's not
asleep."

There she was, sitting up in bed and
smiling at me, and before I knew it I
was scrunched up beside her, telling her
everything – all about the nasty Count
and the feeble Ferdinand and my plan
to scare the pants off them and how it

worked so well and then it worked *too* well and then it all went wrong and I hadn't even known that ferrets *could* swim before but then Jill . . . and now Jill . . .

"Is Jill the big one, with the white fur?"

My mother's voice was too soft, too calm.

"And the red eyes?" she continued.

"And the broken claw on her right front foot . . ."

I looked at her in surprise. Jill had only broken that claw this morning. She'd been trying to dig one of her toys out from a stone gutter she'd wedged it into. How could my mother possibly have known about that?

"Yes, but how . . ." I started to ask her, but the look on her face stopped me with an impossible hope.

". . . like that?"

She was pointing to the foot of the bed. There was only a single candle burning in the room, so at first it was hard to see what she was pointing *at*. But then my eyes cleared and I realised that what had looked like a lump in the bedclothes was, in fact, blinking sleepily at me.

It was Jill. And she was not alone.

She was curled around a heap of tiny brand-new kits. She'd been giving birth while the rest of us had been playing the fool.

Suddenly, there was a gigantic honk that made all of us jump. *What now?!* I thought. But it was only Fat Margaret, standing by the door, blowing her nose.

"I'll just go and tell Warren," she muttered gruffly. "Silly boy's mad about the beasts . . ."

She was trying so hard not to look soft – you had to laugh.

I snuggled in with my mum at the top end of the bed, and Jill and her babies went back to sleep at the bottom end, and it was big sighs of content all round.

"So, my ferret-girl," said my mother

softly, "it's all worked out, after all."

I'm almost positive it was Jill she was talking to ...

WAG
AND THE
KING

Chapter One

Old Dog, New Tricks?

Remember that thing they say?

You can't teach an old dog new tricks.

Ever stop to wonder *why*? If you did, you probably thought it was because old dogs are too stupid, or old dogs are too stiff. Rubbish! Old dogs can't learn new tricks because *they haven't got the time!*

My name's Wag. I'm old, and I'm a dog. And I am SO BUSY keeping my human out of trouble that I have NO TIME LEFT to learn tricks. Old tricks, new tricks, tricks of *any* sort or smell.

Oh, come on, you say. No one can get in *that* much trouble, you say. You *must* be exaggerating.

That's what you say.

Are you right? I don't think so. Take last week, for example . . .

Chapter Two

Apprentice Tom

The Boy's name is Tom, and I've had him ever since his parents left him here, at the Castle, when he was little more than a puppy.

Do you know about apprenticing? If you do, you can skip the rest of this bit. If you don't – this is how it works.

Humans with a big litter apprentice some of them to other humans (called Masters) who are skilled at something the parents don't know much about themselves. The children learn a new trade by watching and helping and being taught, and the Master gets a new assistant. Even the Princes and Princesses get sent away to other castles, to learn things about Kinging and Queening that maybe their own mothers and fathers aren't so good on. It's a pretty sensible system, and mostly it all works out quite well.

Mostly.

In Tom's case, his parents apprenticed him to the Court Minstrel. On the face of it, they couldn't have chosen a better job for their son: no heavy lifting, indoor work, guaranteed invitations to every feast, nice clothes and a warm basket, er, bed to sleep in.

The Master Minstrel was one of the Old King's favourites. The Old King died not so long ago, and his son Roderick was called back from *his* apprenticeship to take over. So now we have a Young King. He's still new at the job and has a lot to learn, but he seems a likeable enough human. *And* he seems to be perfectly happy with his father's Minstrel, so that should be good news for the Boy, too.

It sounds great, doesn't it?

As it worked out, however, it was a bit like apprenticing a Jack Russell to an Irish Wolfhound.

Not exactly the perfect match, if you get what I mean.

Chapter Three

Minstrel Mismatch

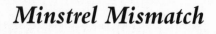

"You CANNOT sing an Ode to the Beauty of Lady Gravel with your eyes crossed and pretending to be sick all the time!" the Master shouted.

"You cannot sing an Ode to the Beauty of Lady Gravel AT ALL!" the Boy shouted back. "Because the Beauty of Lady Gravel doesn't exist!!"

There you have it. It's not that our Tom can't sing – he has quite a nice voice, and we've had many a pleasant howl together of an evening. But when it comes to flattering the Lords and Ladies of the Court with flowery

phrases, or complimenting all the
Royal Relatives in rhyming couplets, or
warbling "The Lament of Lord Stush" –
well, as far as *that* part of the job goes,
the Boy hasn't the nose for it, and no
mistake.

Lord Pompadour his foes did ravage...
...He's no more savage than a cabbage!

85

The Lord, a-weltering in his blood,
Took a long last look at his Lady
And murmured "My Dearest,
  oh my, ah me!
When I'm dead,
  dear Lady,
  remember me!"

And she looked at him,
  and sighed and said,
"All right, but I really do
  not suppose
    That you're going to die
    With a slight black eye
    And a great big fat
      bloody nose!"

You get the idea.

In the course of this morning alone, the Boy had already had a scroll, a roll, and a flagon thrown at him by the Master.

"GET OUT GET OUT GET OUT!" bellowed the Master. "And take that mangy mongrel with you!"

Tom grinned at me. Escape! But then the Master changed his mind.

"NO!" he yelled. "Come back. I've got a better idea."

Uh-oh. The Boy and I exchanged worried looks.

"You can attend the King's Audience instead. And you can *stay there* until you find something *you* deem worthy of singing an Ode about. Don't come back without a finished song. And take the dog."

He could be really mean, the Master.

So there we were, stuck in the Great Hall, listening to a bunch of old poops droning on about drains and taxes and treaties and trade. The only person more bored than us was the Young King.

He kept yawning behind his hand, and playing with his sleeves. (Great long droopy sleeves-to-the-floor was one of the idiot fashions he'd brought back from his apprenticeship at Castle Finicky.) He looked really silly, and really fed up.

Until . . . there was a blare of trumpets that made everybody jump. They only use the trumpets to announce the arrival of *really important* people. So who important would want to show up to an event as dull as this one? I wondered.

I was just about to find out – and when I did, I couldn't stop my tail from wagging like a windmill.

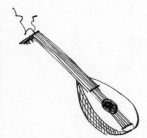

Chapter Four

WOW!

What walked through those big
double doors was an absolute vision
of exotically clipped fur, high-stepping
paws, and the sweetest snout.

Oh, and the human with her wasn't
bad either.

"The Lady Spectacula, Ambassadress
from the Kingdom of Grimm,"
announced the Chamberlain in a
disapproving voice. "Our long-standing
rival. And enemy. And traditional
adversary. Locally known as The
Bad Guys."

The old Chamberlain was definitely

trying to send a message to the Young King, but *he* wasn't receiving. Young Roderick was wearing an utterly goopy expression all over his face. Even Tom looked a little open-mouthed. It probably had to do with the way Lady Spectacula was dressed.

In my opinion, though, something didn't smell right about the Ambassadress, and it wasn't just her perfume. Unfortunately, the King only had a human nose.

"Silence, Chamberlain! How *dare* you be rude to this fair Lady!" he squeaked. Then he got his voice back under control. "You are all dismissed," he said, trying to sound like his father. "I will meet with the Ambassadress from Grimm – alone!"

Well, I wasn't going anywhere with a lady dog like that around, and the Boy was too curious to even consider leaving. So we slid out of sight together behind the throne, and waited while the Great Hall reluctantly emptied.

At last there was a moment's silence, and then a CLICK. We peeked.

The Lady had just finished locking
the big double doors, and was turning
round. She started slinking up the Hall
towards the King like some horrible cat,
smiling at him with a whole mouth full
of little white teeth. The lady dog padded
gracefully along at her embroidered heels.

"Your Majesty," the Lady purred as they
came close. "Thank you so much. For this
opportunity to be alone with you and . . ."

"Mnerg," gargled Roderick.

". . . to END YOUR LIFE!"

You've never seen a dog – or a human – change so fast. All the

sweetness disappeared, lost in snarls,
as the two launched themselves at
the King. The Lady had a knife in
one hand – the lady dog had her

jaws wide – the King threw himself backwards – we leaped out of hiding – and the result was a yelling, snapping scrum on the floor.

Chapter Five

Run! Run!

"*Look out!*"

"GRRRRRRR!!!!!!"

"DIE!! DIE!!"

"Grrrrr – YIP!"

"OWWWW!"

The attackers had evidently *not*
expected any company. Tom made
use of their confusion to tangle the
Grimmian dog up in the Lady's skirts,
while I managed to bite her on the
hand. The knife went flying – and then
so did we!

"This way, Your Majesty!" Tom
yelled, dragging the King by one arm

through the servant's door behind the throne. I could hear the Grimmians struggling to untangle themselves as we slammed it shut, as well as a faint cry of *"Come back, you coward!"*

"Run, Your Majesty!" Tom called over his shoulder as he piled some old boxes against the door to slow the assassins down.

But Roderick was just standing there, staring.

"I never knew there was a door there," he murmured, sounding dazed.

"Come ON!"

We'd barely gone three steps when the King fell over onto his nose. Tom helped him up, and then he was down again.

"Oh these *idiot* sleeves!" muttered the King as he tripped over them yet again.

"What I wouldn't give for some proper clothes and a sword . . ."

I couldn't do anything about the sword, but a dog is as good as his teeth.

RRRIPPPP!

"Great St Bernard! Even your dog's attacking me!"

RRRRRIIIIPPPPP!

I could hear the laughter – and exasperation – in Tom's voice.

"No, Your Highness. Wag's just, um, redesigning your costume. So you won't trip up so much. Or look so much like an idiot. Your Majesty. Sire."

The King spluttered. He was not used to all this, you could tell. Tom tucked the sleeves into his belt and set off again.

"Let's try along here!"

We raced down one of the back corridors, until Tom skidded to a stop.

"We'll hide in here," he said, "till the Guards catch up."

We piled into a disused cupboard. Luckily it was almost empty, because there certainly wasn't a lot of room in there for two humans and a dog. The King managed to crack his head on a shelf a few times, before he learned to stay low.

"Where *are* we?" he panted. "I thought I knew my own Castle!

I certainly thought about it enough when I was away."

"You wouldn't know back here, Your Highness, you being a Prince and all. You'd just know the posh bits. It's the servants and apprentices, people like that, who *really* know a castle." Tom was busy peering through a crack in the door, so he didn't see the look the King gave him. But I did.

Young Roderick was *really* not used to all this.

"Where are the Guards?" muttered Tom. "Why haven't they shown up yet?"

The King turned pink.

"I expect they're still trying to break down the door of the Great Hall. She . . . locked it."

"And you let her."

"I . . . she . . . um . . ."

I whined and made a big thing of putting my nose to the floor. Tom stared at me for a minute, puzzled, and then slapped his forehead.

"Of course – we can't hide here! She'll be using that dog to track us! Come on!"

The King groaned, straightened up too soon, banged his head again, moaned, and then managed to drag himself out into the corridor after us. He'd acquired three cobwebs and an irate spider in his hair, and a generous smudging of dirt, all over.

You had to grin.

"Tell your dog to stop laughing at me," the King growled. "He's no picture of elegance, either."

But there was no time for chat.

I could smell them now – the lady dog and the killer Lady – getting dangerously close. Without a yip, I led the way.

"Where . . . ?" I heard the King begin, but the Boy told him to Shush. And he didn't say Please.

I knew we had to get the Grimmians off our tails soon. I also knew we had to get help – there was *no chance* we could beat them in a straight fight.

Fortunately, I had a plan.

Chapter Six

What's That Smell?

"Ah ha!" said Tom. "Who's a clever dog then?"

We'd arrived, and the Boy seemed to have caught on to my idea right off.

We exchanged glances, and started to move in behind Roderick. But the King didn't notice. He was too busy staring at the midden as if he'd never seen one before – come to think of it, he probably never had – and holding his nose.

"Where are we? What's that smell? What are we doing here? Wha – EEEK!!"

A shove from the Boy and a nip from

me, and the first part of the plan was accomplished. No dog on earth could distinguish the single scent of a King from all the smells of the midden.

"Lie still, Your Majesty," Tom hissed as he covered up the few bits of Monarch that still showed. "We'll be back for you as soon as the coast is clear!"

Then, dragging the King's ripped-off sleeves along the ground to lay a false trail, we were off again.

Round behind the kitchens, past the privy, under the washing lines we went. Our pursuers were gaining on us. This old dog was panting and puffing, and even the Boy's young legs were starting to stumble.

"Nearly ... there ..." I heard him gasp.

Over some barrels, in one door and out another, round a corner – *and there it was!*

THE GUARDHOUSE!!

"Help! Guards! The King ..." yelled Tom with all the breath he had left.

I'll never forget the look on their faces as the Lady and her hound skidded round the last corner seconds later, and saw us ... just us and not a sniff of the King (unless you count a couple of draggled sleeves) – with a

dozen burly guardsmen on either side –
WOOF!!

The Guardsmen piled in, doing
guardsmanly things in a nervous sort
of way – you could tell they weren't
used to dealing with High-Class Female
Threats to the Monarchy, human *or*
dog. But still, in the end, they managed
to get the two bundled away.

And us? Well, for a while we just sat
there on the Guardhouse steps, in the
nice sun, with our tongues hanging out.
Then I noticed that the Boy's expression
was beginning to change. His face went
from looking all red and excited . . . to
looking uneasy . . . to looking pale and
worried sick.

"I can't believe I just shoved the King
in a cupboard, Wag," he muttered.

Yes, but you saved his life, I thought back.

"I can't believe you just ripped the King's sleeves off," he murmured.

Yes, but I saved his life, I thought again.

"I *really* can't believe we just pushed the King into the midden and covered him up with rubbish," he moaned.

Yes, but we really did save his life, I insisted.

Tom didn't hear.

"We are *so* in trouble," he groaned, and buried his head in his hands.

Which is why he didn't immediately see the Monster.

It appeared unannounced from around the corner, and slurped slowly towards us, leaving a trail of pungent vegetable bits in its wake. Potato peelings wreathed its head and shoulders; carrot tops stuck to its feet like seaweed; and strange unidentifiable smudges and stains coloured its body and face.

And then there was the smell . . .

"I take it 'the coast is clear'," it said, in a very flat voice.

Tom's head jerked up.

"Y –Your Majesty," he stammered.

Ah, I thought, *not a Monster then.*

"If the . . . emergency is over, I would like to bathe," continued the Monster – I mean, Monarch. "Kindly inform my valet that I will be in my chambers."

Without waiting for an answer, King

Roderick turned, wetly, and glooped away.

"I am so dead," said Tom. If he'd
had a tail, it would have drooped. He
trudged off in search of the King's valet.

He seemed to want to be by himself
for some reason, so I let him go. There
wasn't anything more I thought I should
be doing, so I turned myself around a
few times, curled up, and went to sleep.

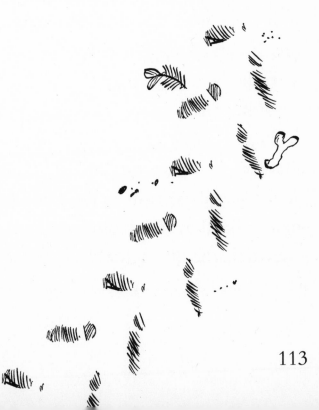

Chapter Seven

The Feast

Several days later, there was a feast
to honour the King's victory over the
Grimmian spy. Unfortunately, the
Master Minstrel had caught a bad cold
in the meantime, and lost his voice
almost completely. There was no way
he would be able to sing!

So that left . . .

"Now remember what I've taught
you, Tom," croaked the Master. "Loud
clear voice, don't rush, and for goodness'
sake, make the King look good!"

He gave the Boy a shove. Tom stumbled
forward into the centre of the Great Hall

115

and stopped dead. The babble of voices carried on around him. He didn't speak. He didn't move. He looked frozen with fear.

There are some moments when a cold wet nose firmly applied to a human's hand is the only way to get them operational.

"AKKK!" squawked Tom. Not the most elegant opening, but at least it got everybody's attention.

The old Chamberlain rose to his feet and announced, "Your Majesty. Lords and Ladies. Due to the Master Minstrel's unfortunate illness, his apprentice will sing for us tonight, on the subject of King Roderick's Recent Heroic Victory Over the Evil Grimmian Assassin."

Another application of the cold-and-wet got the Boy strumming. As I looked around at the audience I could see a

range of expressions, from complete
indifference to polite interest. The King,
of course, had had lots of practice not
showing his feelings on his face, but I
could see one of his feet under the table.

It was tapping nervously.

The Boy's voice was a bit wobbly, but
it *was* loud, and more or less in tune.

"A minstrel's task is to tell the tale
Of the Mighty Deeds of the Great.

I'm here to sing, to one and all,
The dire events that did befall
Our Sovereign King in his Audience Hall
And . . ."

He paused. He strummed a few
chords, then nodded, as if he'd made
up his mind about something. Then he
began to sing again.

But there had been a change.

". . . And the truth is what I'll tell."

The King's foot froze, and he sat
forward a little in his throne. All through
the Great Hall there was an uneasy
rustle of expensive clothes. But the Boy
didn't seem to notice. It was almost as if
he were singing to himself.

119

120

Then she lunged with her dagger!
The King leapt in the air
But - lucky for him! -
This Old Dog was still there!

121

And I tell you the truth,
And the truth that I say
Is that this Old Dog
Was the Hero that day!

As a rule, dogs don't blush. But when he said that, and everyone looked at me – well, I certainly got hot under the collar.

124

And meanwhile our Monarch
Was coming to grief
Because, as he scarpered,
He tripped on his sleeve.

125

The Great Hall was so still you
could have heard a flea hop. As the
tale unfolded, there were open mouths
wherever you looked, and the King was
as pale as a bowl of milk.

=129

132

That was the end. There was a moment of deeply, truly horrified silence after Tom stopped playing. Nobody breathed.

Then . . .

"That's not the truth, you know," said the King quietly.

Chapter Eight

Fired!

A babble of voices exploded around us.

"Well of course it isn't the truth!"

"No one would believe such a thing!"

"The *idea*!"

"The boy should be flogged!"

"Outrageous!"

King Roderick raised his hand and the noise stopped short.

"I know it's not the truth," he continued, "because I was there. I *know* what happened. And I know it wasn't just the dog who saved me."

There was another, more uncertain pause. The courtiers were confused. But the King wasn't.

"It was *you* too," he said to Tom. "*That's* the truth." He raised his voice a little, to make sure that everyone could hear. "I was very, very stupid. And an apprentice boy and a dog saved my life."

His eyes hadn't left us.

"You could have made something up, you know. To make me look good.

That's what minstrels are supposed to do, isn't it? But you didn't. Why didn't you? Is it because you don't like me? Or *don't you want to be a minstrel?*"

The Boy scuffed his shoes about in the rushes for a bit, and then muttered,

"I like the singing. And the stories. I like telling stories. But –" and here his voice got so quiet the King and

the entire Court had to lean forward to hear him – "I like the stories to be true."

There was another pause. Then the elderly Chamberlain coughed.

"Yes, Chamberlain?" said the King politely.

"I have a suggestion, Sire," the old man wheezed.

The King nodded encouragingly.

"And my suggestion is this. Sack the apprentice minstrel. He obviously isn't fit for the job."

Tom's face fell; my tail drooped. He was going to be sent away! I'd never see him again!

But the old man wasn't finished.

"Give him a new job," he continued. "Let him be your Fool."

Some of the younger courtiers looked blank, but *I* remembered the Old King's Fool. He'd been like an unofficial advisor for years, until he got too wobbly on his legs and went to live out his days in the country. He'd always dressed his advice up in wild jokes and stories. But I remember the Old King always listened . . .

"My what?" said the Young King.

"Your Fool, Sire. It's an old custom, having one person in Court who will always speak the truth to the powerful," the Chamberlain explained. "It doesn't mean he can just go about being rude, though. Oh no. His truth has to be dressed in stories and songs and jokes. But he has your permission *never to have to lie*. Oh, and he has to wear a special costume: a funny hat, and bells on his trousers, and a multi-coloured shirt, and he carries around a stick with lots of ribbons – that sort of thing."

"In other words, he gets to dress up like an idiot," laughed the King. Then he became serious again. "Would you like to do this, Tom? Would you like to be my Fool?"

I held my breath. *Don't go away, Boy!* I thought at him as hard as I could. *Take the job! Take the job!*

He put a hand on my head and gave me a long, serious look. Then he squared his shoulders, and spoke to the King.

"The answer is yes, Your Majes . . . Roderick. I would be happy to be your Fool. We both would – I, *and* Wag."

The King nodded solemnly.

"Of course," he said.

141

Chapter Nine

Old Dog, New Job

Well? I told you I wasn't exaggerating. I really AM too busy just trying to keep the Boy out of trouble. Learn new tricks, ha! NO TIME.

But he's got this new job now, you say. He can't possibly get into any more trouble *now*.

That's what you say.

And I say . . .

PULL THE OTHER THREE –

THEY'VE GOT BELLS ON!

THE
MUCKER'S
TALE

Chapter One

The Wizard and the Sweeper Boy

The ragged boy leaned on his broom and sighed as the wizard walked past. Once again, he hadn't had the nerve

to speak to the old man, to ask him the questions that filled his mind day and night . . .

KABOOM!

The wizard had just started up the steps to his magnificent house when the street shook and a cloud of smelly purple smoke billowed out of the front door. He turned around quickly and went back down again.

He noticed that a ragged boy with a broom was watching him, and he smiled.

"I think I'll just sit out on the steps for a bit, and let that settle," the wizard said to him. "Perhaps you'd like to join me?"

The ragged boy's eyes went very big, but he came over anyway and sat down beside the wizard.

"What's your name?" the old man

asked. He was wearing a fabulously pointy hat and fancy robes and had a spectacularly long white beard, but he had a kind voice.

"They call me Sweeper, Honoured Sir," the boy said. "Because that's my job. I sweep the streets."

The old man chuckled. "You know what they used to call me when I was your age?" he said. "Mucker!"

The boy couldn't believe it. "You mean – you weren't always a wizard?" he exclaimed.

"Oh no – not by a long shot! Once I was just a stable boy, and nobody called me 'Honoured Sir'! No, like I said, everybody called me 'Mucker'!"

And the wizard's mind went back to those long ago days and, as Sweeper listened, he began to tell a story . . .

Chapter Two

Kingdom in the Sky

"Hey, Mucker!"

Oh yes, that was me. I grew up in a tiny kingdom, hidden so high in the mountains that the clouds kept bumping into the castle walls. From as soon as I was tall enough to handle a broom, I'd been the stable boy.

151

The castle stable wasn't very big, but it still needed a lot of sweeping because, as you know, all horses are really, really good at producing manure. And once it's been produced, somebody has to muck it all out, and that somebody was me.

I didn't mind. Not too much, anyway.

Because the horses I was sweeping up after weren't just *ordinary* horses. Not by a long shot. *Our* horses could *fly*.

You don't see flying horses much outside the mountains. They are creatures of the cold, feeding on meadow grass and pine trees and thriving in the frigid air. Also, although they *can* take off from a flat running start, they much prefer a decent launching cliff to get airborne, and they are at their best with the kind of savage winds that batter round mountain peaks like ours.

You might say I was really lucky, getting to work with such fabulous animals. And I was! But the problem was, there was something I wanted to do even more.

I wanted to be a wizard.

And I wasn't the only one.

Even though our kingdom was small and out of the way, it still had everything a kingdom *should* have. We had an extremely honourable King (who was, sadly, a widower), a collection of Courtiers, some Faithful Old Retainers, the bravest of brave Guardsmen, a deliciously talented Cook, a Court Wizard (whose name was "Magnus the Magnificent") . . . and a Princess. Her name was Emmeline.

You might say *she* was really lucky, too, being a Princess. But there was something she wanted to be doing, even more than princessing, just like me. She wanted to be a wizard too.

We used to meet up in the stables and complain about our lives. (Emmeline was as good with the flying horses as I was. She would practise her singing on

them and brush the gunk out of their tails and lend a hand when my two just weren't enough. She was also teaching me to read, as I had no time for proper schooling.)

"My father makes me take singing lessons and history lessons and algebra lessons, but he won't let me take lessons from Magnus the Magnificent," moaned Emmeline. "He says princesses don't need to know how to do magic."

"Same here," I moaned back. "Stable boys don't need to know how to do magic either."

"I don't think he'll ever change his mind," sighed Emmeline. "*Nothing* ever changes around here."

"Nothing ever changes, and nothing ever happens," I sighed back.

And it really did feel like that. It felt as if everything would stay just the way it was for at least a hundred million years. Until, one day, something *did* happen, and *everything* changed.

That was the day the raiders came . . .

Chapter Three

The Day the Raiders Came

It wasn't as if we didn't have walls and gates and the bravest of Guardsmen. We did. But not even the oldest Old Retainer could remember a time when anyone had tried to *attack* us. Being small and remote, pretty much on the top of the world, had kept us safe and unnoticed for, well, forever. But all that was about to change.

The rotten raiders got into the castle by pretending to be a travelling merchant and his servants. Goodness knows what the Guardsmen thought they'd be selling, so far off the beaten

track. Whatever it was, the gates were
opened and in they came, as easy as
anything. Then, the moment they were
safely inside our walls, they pulled out
more daggers and swords than we had
in out entire armoury – *and they grabbed
Princess Emmeline!*

"Get everyone into the Throne Room NOW!" snarled the leader, a scrawny, straw-haired man with pale, mean eyes. "And if you value this little missy, you won't take all day about it, either!"

Word spread like fire and soon every soul in the castle had gathered in the Throne Room, from the oldest Retainer to the King himself. I could barely get in through the door, the room was so packed, but I managed to climb up on a chest to see over everybody's heads. And there was Emmeline, with one of the henchmen gripping her roughly by the arm, her face pale but her back straight.

The King turned to the leader.

"May we know the name of the man who is treating a Princess with so little respect?" he said in a deep voice.

"You don't *know* who I am?" The

leader of the ruffians seemed astonished, and his henchmen pulled shocked faces. "Well, what can you expect from a bunch of hill-fools? Allow me to educate you. I am Prince Franck."

"Indeed?" said the King, making it clear that he was not much impressed by this. "And what is it you want with my daughter?"

Prince Franck laughed, but he turned an angry red too.

"What, this little no-nothing two-a-penny mountain princess? I don't want her at all, except as a hostage!" he sneered. He began to strut

up and down as he talked. I couldn't help noticing how skinny his legs were. He looked a lot like a chicken parading around like that, but somehow it didn't seem very funny just then.

"No, I'm here for something much more valuable. Something that is going to change the future of a *proper* kingdom – *mine!*"

The King said, "Didn't you say you were only a prince?"

"A prince – for *now*. My father is an old man. He won't last much longer."

"Hasn't he chosen his heir?"

"Oh, he's chosen all right." Franck's voice was venomous. "He's chosen my brother to get everything after his death."

"So that is that, surely." The King was an honourable man. You could see he really didn't understand anyone like the Prince at all.

"Yeah, right," Franck sneered, and his men snorted and made rude faces.

What does he want? I thought. I couldn't believe this was really happening. *If he doesn't want Emmeline, what's he after?*

Then Prince Franck spoke again and it all became horribly clear.

"I'm here to take your flying horses," he announced. "I'm going to take them, every last one, and I'm going to fly them over my brother's castles and drop bombs until everyone's dead or they make *me* the king. Oh, and unless you, and every man and woman you're the king of, vows not to do one single, solitary thing to stop me, I'll kill your daughter."

Chapter Four

The Vile Prince Franck

There was a horrified gasp, and then silence. There could be no argument with this ghastly excuse for a prince.

"Good. Very sensible," Franck sneered. "Now, I can't be bothered taking an oath off this lot one at a time." And he waved a dismissive hand at us all. Then he turned to our King. "But if *you* take the vow for everybody, they'll have to obey you. That's how it works with us royalty, doesn't it." And he smirked and squirmed in a way that obviously made our King want to go away and have a bath.

Nevertheless he said, "Give me back my daughter, and you have my word, that no man I am king of will try to stop you."

"*Or* woman!" Franck cried. "You'll not catch me out with that old trap! Say it straight, and no tricks."

Our King, who would never have considered anything tricksy or underhanded in a hundred years, gave him a look of deep scorn, but repeated the oath again anyway.

"No man or woman that I am King of will try to stop you. You have my word. Give me back my daughter."

Prince Franck stared round the room, a big stupid grin of triumph on his face, and then flicked a finger at the thug holding the Princess.

"Let her go. We don't need *her* any more!"

The henchman laughed and gave Princess Emmeline a shove forward. She staggered, but didn't fall. For a moment I thought our King was going to punch the man in the face, but with an effort he restrained himself. He wasn't supposed to do things like that, being royal. He probably wanted to give his daughter a big hug too, but he didn't.

"Go to your room now, my dear," he said to her instead, gentle but firm, and with her back still as straight as a tree, the Princess went.

I slipped out of the room after her.
"Princess?"

She turned on me so fast I had to
jump back. Her face was furious. "He
sent me to my room! Like a useless
child! Our beautiful horses are going
to be stolen away and all I'm good for
is to be a hostage – and then get sent

to my room! Well, I won't have it. We're going to *stop* those thieving knaves."

I was shocked. "But we *can't*!" I said. "Your father agreed, on his honour, that no man or woman in the kingdom would lift a finger to stop them."

"That's right," snapped Emmeline. "And we're neither. We're children. Come on!"

We ran as fast as we could, by the back ways right up to the top of the main tower, the one that looks down into the courtyard. The stables opened off from that courtyard, so it was the best place to get an idea of what was going on. It was a long climb, and we were both out of breath by the time we got there.

"We should be able to see what's happening," I whispered to the Princess, "but we must be careful they don't see *us*."

She nodded, and together we crept to the parapet and peered over.

I don't know what I thought I was going to see – it could hardly have been anything good! – but I was totally unprepared for the scene that lay below.

The sound of shouts and cursing was

loud and painfully clear. The courtyard was full of great wooden cages on wheels, with teams of oxen yoked to them. The raiders must have left them just out of sight down the road, but now they'd been dragged up, and they were loading our flying horses into them. But the cowards were taking no chances.

It hurt like a punch in the stomach to see our horses like that, blindfolded and haltered and with their beautiful wings tied to their sides with ropes.

They had never known even an unkind word – how could they understand being treated like this? The thought of them dragged away to the hot flatlands in the hands of men like Franck made me want to race down and, and . . . and what?

173

I didn't realise I'd started shaking until the Princess put her hand on my arm and drew me back from the edge.

"Thank goodness the colts are out in the far meadow," she said. "That's at least something. Now, we need to think . . . what are we going to do?"

I stared at her, feeling absolutely desperate. All I could think about was how there wasn't a man or woman in the entire kingdom who could stop the horrible Prince and his wretched raiders from stealing those horses. There was only *us* – and at that moment I couldn't see what we could *possibly* do.

But Emmeline had no doubts.

"Come on, Mucker – don't you see? It's just like in the stories," she whispered, her eyes shining. "When it looks as if all is lost, and anyone who *could* save the day *can't*, and there's only the most unlikely people left, and they discover that they have *the one special thing* that's the only *possible* way to beat the baddies."

I tried to interrupt, but she was still talking.

"The most unlikely people – that would definitely be us. And the one special thing . . . but what would *that* be? Think, Emmeline, think! All those princessing lessons I've had – all that singing and history and algebra – oh, why didn't I learn anything *useful*?!

Never mind, it'll come to us, I know it will. We'll think on the way. Let's go!"

She was already up and starting for the stairs, but I called her back.

"Princess! No! Wait!"

She paused. "What is it? There's no time to lose – come *on*!"

I shook my head. "No, not yet. We can't go after them yet – we'd be spotted right away. There's no cover for the first part of that road. We need to let

176

them get ahead, wait till they stop for the night . . ."

With a big sigh, she came back. "You're right, I guess. But I hate like anything letting them just *go*!"

"I know. I hate it too." But my mind wasn't completely on her just at that moment. "It's a good thing we're both titchy," I muttered.

She stiffened. "What did you just call me?!"

"I called you titchy. Which is a good thing. A grown person would be too heavy for the colts."

Maybe it was a bad idea . . .

Then her eyes went wide. "We're going to follow on the colts! You're a genius! It's the perfect way to catch up with the raiders."

"We still don't know what we'll do

when we get there," I said.

But I could tell she wasn't listening to me any more.

"I'll meet you back here in a bit," she said. "There's something I've got to get . . ."

Chapter Five

The One Special Thing

The raiders were long gone by the time the Princess returned. She was out of breath and clutching a heavy bundle in her arms.

"What . . . ?" I asked but she'd already started to unpack.

"Jackets." (Nobody flies in the mountains wearing just indoor clothes.) "Gloves. Some food. And . . . the one special thing!"

She had a big triumphant grin all over her face.

"What is it?" I asked.

"Magnus the Magnificent's spell

book!" she
crowed.

"But
... but ...
you *stole* it?!"
I stammered.

She shrugged.
"Just borrowed. We'll
give it back afterwards."

I looked at the book doubtfully. It
was big and impressive and black, with
stars on the cover, and complicated
looking writing on the inside.

"You know ... I can't read very well
yet ..." I muttered.

"But I can!" cried Emmeline. "Let's
go!"

The castle was as stirred up as an
anthill, with people rushing around
and whispering in shocked little groups

and then rushing around some more. We were almost noticed a dozen times over, but at last we made it to the back gate and panted up the mountainside towards the far meadow.

The colts weren't ready for saddles yet, or bridles either. I was worried it would take forever to catch any – they could be very skittish and tended to treat everything as a game of tag. But I needn't have worried. As soon as the colts heard us coming, they came trotting up, and Princess Emmeline was immediately surrounded by soft noses and feathery wings.

"Which two shall we take?" she asked.

"Hiho for me," I said, pointing. "And Piddler for you. They're the strongest. I only hope the rest won't decide to

come as well – they never want to miss
out on anything."

The Princess was already on Piddler's
back. She settled herself between his
wings as the colt pranced about, and
called to me,

"Hurry up! It's time we were off."

She'd urged her steed into a run and
was heading for the launching cliff

before I'd even put a hand on Hiho. I
scrambled up and we raced after her –
trailing the rest of the herd who, as I'd
feared, had no intention of being left
out of whatever adventure was on offer.
As Hiho reached the edge and dropped
off into the sky, there was Emmeline
on Piddler, catching the up draught,
swooping away, laughing in excitement.

The colts didn't care where we were
going – they were having too much fun.
The sun was beginning to set behind
the mountains as we reached the place
where the road entered the forest. There
was a clearing not too far along that,
if I'd guessed right, the raiders would
use to overnight in, so I headed for
the other side of the trees. There was a
place there that had a spring and good
pasture for the colts and enough height

184

so we could use it to launch from when they needed to take off again.

The moment we landed, the colts wasted no time beginning to graze, and Emmeline and I headed off stealthily into the forest.

"Remember, I don't exactly know what I'm doing," she whispered to me. "We need to get really close if my magic's going to work."

"As close as we can, without being spotted," I said.

It was getting dark under the trees, but I saw her nod. Then she grabbed my arm and pointed.

A light was flickering up ahead. It was a cooking fire. We had found the raiders' camp.

Franck and his men *had* decided to spend the night in the clearing. As we crept closer, we could see them moving about, making dinner, squabbling about who got to sit on which log. Prince Franck was complaining loudly about not having a proper feather bed to sleep in. There was no sign of the oxen. They must have pastured them away from their camp. (We were lucky not to have stumbled upon them – oxen

are noisy creatures when startled.) The raiders had kept their stolen property in plain view, though. The cages with the flying horses were parked over to one side of the clearing. The horses had been packed in so tightly that there wasn't room for them to lie down, and I could hear the occasional sound as they shifted slightly, trying to find some comfort. I could feel myself starting to shake with anger again, but I pushed it aside. It wasn't time for that.

It was time for Emmeline!

"Ready?" I murmured.

She gave me a thumbs up.

"Ready!" she whispered back.

She could barely see the book but it didn't stop her getting stuck in. She began to whisper and wave her hands about. It looked just like the real thing!

"I'm pretty sure this spell will make those logs they're sitting on burst into flames," she muttered. "Let's see how they like *that*!"

Logs, fire – she did it all right. Unfortunately, it was the logs on the raiders' cooking fire that blazed up, *not* the ones they were sitting on. The only effect of that was the brigands getting their dinner in record time.

She turned the pages, and got ready to try again.

"Right, then, this time I'm putting a sleeping spell on them," whispered Emmeline. "I'll make them sleep for a hundred years. A thousand years. I know I can get this one . . . You just watch."

We did watch, waiting for the men to start to nod, willing their eyes to close. And they *did* close. But the spell only half-worked. One eye per raider drooped shut, so that they were all winking.

"Hey – you trying to be funny?!" snarled one.

"Who do you think you're winking at?!" spat another.

"Do you want a punch in the nose?" snorted a third.

For a few moments I wondered if perhaps they might start fighting

amongst themselves, and solve our
problem that way, but the spell wore off
too fast for that. Grumbling under their
breath, the raiders settled down to their
meal again.

When I looked at Emmeline, she
was already murmuring the words of
yet another enchantment. When it was
finished, she turned to me and hissed,
"This time I didn't hold back. No more
being nice. *That* was a summoning
spell. Any minute now, this clearing is

going to be swarming with ferocious wild wolves and bears, and they're going to tear those raiders to pieces before you can say Grrr. Any minute now!"

When we heard the rustling, we looked at each other in wild delight. I thought, *She's really done it!* And wild animals *did* appear. Just not exactly the animals she'd had in mind . . .

I've never seen squirrels look so confused. Luckily for them, the spell wore off before they actually got to the attacking part. Most of the raiders didn't even notice them, though one yelped, "Aaargh – a rat!" and jumped several feet into the air before pretending he was just practising fight moves.

Defeated, we crawled away.

"It didn't work!" Emmeline whimpered when we got back to the colts, waiting at the forest's edge. "Not a single spell! Magic *wasn't* the one special thing, but what else *can* be?! There's nothing I know about that's any good!"

Piddler came up to give Emmeline's hair a nibble. I tried to shoo him away, thinking she might not feel like being chewed on just then, but only succeeded

in startling him, and he reacted in the
way startled colts do – especially ones
called Piddler. He wee-ed nervously – I
only just got my foot out of the way
in time. I still had that foot in mid-air
when the idea struck.

"There's one thing we haven't tried,"
I said quietly. "One thing that *I* know

about, better than anything else."

Emmeline looked puzzled. "I don't understand. What do you know better than anything else?"

I leaned over and whispered one word.

"Muck."

For a moment she looked as if she thought I'd gone crazy, or was suddenly being randomly rude – and then you could see it all come clear in her mind.

"Genius!" she said.

Let me explain. With any animal or pet that lives with people, the first thing you need to do is to house-train it – you need to teach it to not go to the loo indoors. With a flying horse, however, the thing you want to teach it first is not go to the loo *in mid-air*. There's a word you use to tell them to wait, and

another word for when they've landed
and it's safe to, um, let go.

That second word would be our
special thing!

 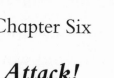 

Chapter Six

Attack!

It was a full moon that night, so
everything was weird-looking in black
and white. All around us, pairs of eyes
glittered strangely, as the colts milled
about, catching our excitement.

The raiders would be asleep by now.
It was time.

We mounted and, as one, the troop
turned towards the edge of the meadow

and began to run . . .

Over the trees we flew to the clearing. Looking down on the sleeping raiders and their evil cages, I could feel my anger boiling up again and this time, I let it through. With all my might, I shouted the word. The colts snorted and jinked in surprise – they couldn't believe I really meant it! So I yelled it again, even louder this time, and Emmeline joined in. The men below s at up, bewildered by the noise – and then . . .

The first few splats landed harmlessly on the ground.

"What's happening?" yelled one raider.

"Is it starting
to rain?" shouted
another.

"What's that
smell?!" wailed a
third.

Then the colts started to get
lucky.

"Aaargh –
something horrible
just landed on
my head!!"

"Yuck – wet –
squishy – HELP!!"

"This rain doesn't smell right!"

The colts were really getting into
it now, making every pass across the
clearing count. Neighing shrilly in
excitement, they swooped back and
forth, bombing the raiders with first-

grade muck and more wet wee than you'd have believed possible. What a nightmare!

The men must have thought things couldn't get worse.

Which is when the cages began to explode.

The adult horses, hearing the cries of the colts, thought their young ones were in danger and went mad. Screaming, frantic, they began to kick, and kick . . . the wood of the cages shattered outward in jagged, cutting shards, spiking anyone within range.

It was chaos – the darkness was full of unseen enemies, noxious, splatting bombs, terrible screams, and skewering sharp wooden things. Prince Franck was screeching contradictory orders – his men yelled and swore, wiping our secret

weapon off their heads and slipping in it as they staggered about.

And then, they all just *cracked*. The entire raiding party ran off into the forest in every direction, crashing through the undergrowth trailing curses and cries, with a few of the colts in pursuit, their shrill neighs spurring them on. Prince Franck's voice howled above all the rest, wailing over and over, "*It's not fair! It's just not FAIR!*"

It was wonderful!

We landed in the clearing, crowing and laughing in delight, thinking we'd really done it this time. Thinking that the danger was all over.

But it wasn't.

The adult horses didn't know their tormentors were gone. Freed from the terrible cages, they were blindly searching for the raiders, desperate to kick and kill, unable to tell enemy from friend. We were in immediate danger – and so were *they*. Unable to see, without their wings to balance, completely disorientated, there was every chance they might crash into one another or run into a tree or fall and break their legs. I didn't know what to do. I just stood there like a noodle, but not Emmeline.

She began to sing.

She'd said before that singing wasn't useful, but she was absolutely wrong. At that moment, it was the one special thing that could reach through all their red rage and speak to the horses. Speak directly to their hearts.

As she sang, the screaming and plunging gradually slowed until the huge creatures had all come to a halt.

Quivering and sweating, they stood still and let us move among them, untying their blindfolds and stroking their necks. The colts helped too, whickering and nuzzling up to their parents, reassuring them they were safe, and that it was all over now.

At last the entire herd had calmed down enough that we were able to lead them away from the clearing to the clean grass, cool spring water – and fresher air! – of the hillside. It would be time to fly them all home again soon, but first we let them drink and graze and roll in the moonlit grass to their hearts' content.

It was a lovely sight.

"We did it," I said happily to Emmeline.

"We really did," she smiled.

Chapter Seven

The Wizards' House

Back on the steps of the Wizard House, Sweeper had hung on every word. But, as the old man came to the end of his tale, the boy frowned.

"But . . . how did all that help you become a wizard?" he asked.

"Well, I'll tell you," the wizard said. "The disaster was over. No one ever saw Prince Franck or his horrible henchmen in the mountains again. The King may have had doubts about just how honourable it had been, the way his daughter and his stable boy got round the vow he'd made, but he was so happy to have everyone safe and his beautiful flying horses home again that he kept those thoughts to himself. He was *so* happy, in fact, and grateful, that he declared a holiday for the whole kingdom, extra oats for all the horses, and anything our hearts desired for Emmeline and me. Well, we didn't need to think very long or hard before we knew exactly what we would ask for. Can you guess?"

"Wizarding lessons!" said the ragged boy with a big grin. "I bet you asked for wizarding lessons!"

The old man laughed. "You're right! Funny how things work out. If it hadn't been for Prince Franck, I might not be here today talking to you."

Suddenly the whole street shook again, and more stinky, purple smoke came billowing out of the wizard's front door. It was closely followed by a white-haired woman with scorch marks on her robes.

"Phew! That was exciting!" she exclaimed as she rubbed soot onto her nose. "Who's your young friend there, my dear?"

"This is Sweeper," the old man said. "I've been telling him about the old days, when we were young. And, unless

I'm mistaken, I think he'd like to be a wizard almost as much as we did, way back then!"

The ragged boy was speechless, but his eyes shone.

The old lady smiled and laughed. "That's grand. But shouldn't you introduce me first?"

"Of course, of course. Sweeper, allow me to introduce my fellow wizard and my wife – Emmeline. Look, the smoke's almost cleared. Let's all go in for tea."